It was late, but Tobyn Wolfe didn't care.

She climbed down the rickety, old fire escape attached to her bedroom window and jumped the last few feet to the ground, her skirt flying up and showing too much of everything, but luckily there was no one around to see. She had on black fishnet stockings with her black skirt, and a black jacket over her shredded black tank top. The only color on her body was the blue streak in her short, curly afro, and she liked that everything about her blended into the night. She turned up the music in her headphones and couldn't help but sing along, loudly, as she jogged to the end of her alley and then the end of her block, waiting at the bus stop to catch the one that would take her to her sister's apartment.

Tobyn didn't care about the stares she got when she sang out loud in public. In fact, she welcomed them. She loved to be the center of attention—loved to be looked at and watched. It was why she'd first joined the Harlem High Notes, the a cappella group at school. And it was why she dreamed about being famous—recording an album and going on tour—why she wanted it all so badly.

The ride passed quickly. When she got to her stop, Tobyn stepped off the bus with her songbook (a worn notebook full of her original lyrics) in one hand and her phone in the other. She texted her sister, **Walking**, as she

FLYY GIRLS

TOBYN: THE IT GIRL

BY ASHLEY WOODFOLK

PENGUIN WORKSHOP

TO EVERY GIRL HOPING TO FIND HER VOICE—AW

YOUR DREAMS WILL ALWAYS TAKE YOU FARTHER
THAN YOUR WHAT-IFS—ZS

PENGUIN WORKSHOP
An imprint of Penguin Random House LLC, New York

First published in the United States of America by Penguin Workshop,
an imprint of Penguin Random House LLC, New York, 2021

Text copyright © 2021 by Ashwin Writing LLC
Illustrations copyright © 2021 by Penguin Random House LLC

Cover illustration by Zharia Shinn

Visit us online at penguinrandomhouse.com.

Library of Congress Control Number: 2021007547

Printed in Canada

ISBN 9780593096109 (pbk)   10 9 8 7 6 5 4 3 2 1 FRE
ISBN 9780593096116 (hc)   10 9 8 7 6 5 4 3 2 1 FRE

started down the block that led to Devyn's apartment. She was actually on time for once, so she knew her sister wouldn't be expecting her yet. The thought of catching Devyn off guard gave Tobyn a little thrill. She liked being underestimated. She liked surprising people, and she loved being surprised, too.

Noelle Lee had surprised Tobyn. They were friends and had been for years. But ever since Noelle had placed her wide palms on either side of Tobyn's face and kissed her after the fall showcase last semester, Tobyn couldn't get her friend's hands out of her head.

Noelle's hands were dark-skinned and long-fingered and bigger than Tobyn's. They were cello hands, perfect for moving along the instrument's long neck, and her nails were always painted (by Lux) so they looked like works of art. Tobyn had tiny hands with short, stubby fingers that gripped a microphone fine but weren't elegant at all. As she walked, Tobyn thought about her hands holding Noelle's, how her lighter brown skin would look next to the deep ebony of her friend's. Things had been fine between them for the last couple of months; calm, and easy, and oddly normal. But it didn't change the fact that Tobyn thought about Noelle way more than she used to. And she didn't know what, if anything, she should do about that.

It was a school night, but lately Tobyn cared less and less about staying out. With her mom working the night shift, it was easy to get away with doing whatever she wanted. She used the fire escape to leave so that her keys would be in the dish by the front door just in case her mom came home earlier than she expected. Climbing the fire escape and sneaking in through her bedroom window meant she could get into bed without needing to pass her mother's bedroom, or opening the creaky front door. She went to shows as if she'd already graduated, not making it home until the sun was rising, like she didn't need to be at Augusta Savage School of the Arts a few hours later. And she drank *a lot* of coffee to keep it all together.

Outside Devyn's building, Tobyn lifted her finger to her sister's buzzer just as a tall guy pushed his way through the door. He held it open for her, so she eased inside with her hand against the wall. She tapped her fingers along the railing as she skipped up the three flights that led to Devyn's apartment, humming along with the song playing in her headphones.

She knocked and waited. Knocked again and waited longer. It was the first time she was hanging out with Devyn in forever, and she was excited but nervous. She and her sister used to be really close, but over the last year Tobyn had felt more and more space opening up between them. Tobyn wondered if Devyn had forgotten about their plans tonight, like she had when Tobyn told her about the fall showcase back in November, and when Tobyn had saved for months and bought two tickets to a show their favorite band was performing on New Year's Eve. It wouldn't be the first time her sister let her down, but it made a part of her heart ache to think it might be happening again.

She took out her phone and sent Devyn another text. **Yo I'm here.** After what seemed like far too long, and still with no one coming to answer the door, Tobyn tried the knob. It turned easily and slid open.

"Hello? Dev?" Tobyn called into the apartment.

It opened into a short hallway, and the living room was on the right, the kitchen on the left. "Anyone home?"

Devyn's head poked out of the living room. Her hair was all fuzzy, streaked with red instead of blue like Tobyn's. (Devyn had added the streak of blue to Tobyn's hair. Whenever she needed a touch-up, Tobyn would text Dev. When her sister stopped by and tilted her head over the small bathroom sink to bleach the roots and reapply the sky-colored dye, it made Tobyn feel like things between them might get back to how they used to be.)

"Oh, hey," Devyn said. Her eyes looked sleepy, and her lids seemed heavier than they normally were, but Devyn walked over to her sister and wrapped her in a bear hug. Devyn kissed Tobyn's forehead and spun her around before they bumped their hips together; a little dance they'd been doing to greet each other since they were small.

"Sorry I'm early," Tobyn said, smirking. "Surprised you, right?"

"You could say that," Devyn agreed.

"We still going out?" Tobyn asked. She looked at her sister's clothes, which seemed like something she'd wear to bed. She glanced at her sister's sleepy eyes again. "I thought you had tickets to a show?"

"Oh yeah," Devyn said, like she was just remembering. "Sorry, I've been kinda hungover all day." They'd been talking about checking out this singer/songwriter for weeks, since they first heard she'd be playing a show at the club around the corner from Devyn's place. Tobyn took a few deep breaths to hide her frustration.

Tobyn looked around the apartment. It was messier than usual, and her sister, who normally loved getting all dressed up and going out, wasn't ready. She didn't even have her contacts in yet, so she was squinting at her phone. Tobyn grabbed Devyn's hand.

"Dev, you good? Everything okay?"

Devyn's eyes seemed distracted. She pulled her hand away. "Yeah, of course. Everything's fine."

Tobyn didn't believe her. The Wolfe women—their mother, Sabrina, Tobyn, and Devyn—were all stubbornly good at keeping secrets. It was why Tobyn never showed anyone her song book. Tobyn knew it was why their mother never talked about their father. And it was why Devyn was lying now. So instead of trying to force the truth out of her sister, Tobyn said, "Soooo . . . I think I have a crush on Noelle."

"What?" Devyn replied with a smile. "You serious?"

Tobyn nodded. "Remember I told you she kissed me?"

"Uh, how could I forget?" Devyn said.

Tobyn laughed. "Well, ever since then, I don't know. I just think about her more. Differently."

Devyn bit her bottom lip and grinned. Tobyn thought she looked more like herself in that moment—like she did on stage with her band: mischievous, brave, and ready to show the best parts of herself to the world.

"Follow your heart, little sis. This is the only life you get," Devyn said, and then, "Oh, wait, I got you something."

Devyn pulled a small box out of her dresser drawer and handed it to Tobyn. "What's this for?" Tobyn asked.

"Just open it," Devyn said. She bounced on her tippy toes.

Inside, Tobyn found a small charm bracelet

with a shiny gold microphone dangling from one of the links. "Whoa," Tobyn said. "This is beautiful."

"I saw it and had to get it," Devyn told her. "It's so you."

"This looks expensive. You sure you can afford it? It's been awhile since the band had a big gig, right?" Devyn's band, Boys Behaving Badly, had been getting better and better, but recently Devyn had been oddly quiet whenever Tobyn asked if they had any gigs coming up.

Devyn waved her off. "Doesn't matter. I've been singing on the subway like we used to, to make a little extra cash. Besides, I want you to have something to remember me by."

"Remember you by?" Tobyn said, frowning.

Devyn hesitated for a second, but then she laughed. "You know. When you go away for school."

"Oh," Tobyn said. "Well, I don't even know if I'm going to college next year. But you don't have to buy me things, Dev. We could just hang out more."

Devyn picked at a hole in her shorts. "Sometimes I wonder if hanging out with you at all is a good idea."

Tobyn slipped the bracelet out of the box and onto her wrist. It was a perfect fit. "What does that mean?" Tobyn asked.

"Nothing," Devyn said, shaking her head. She reached out, touched the tiny microphone, and glanced up at Tobyn, who smiled.

"This bracelet is so freaking cute," Tobyn said, lifting her arm to look at it more closely. "You the best," she said.

"Glad ya like it," Devyn said.

Tobyn sat on Devyn's bed and watched her sister get dressed. Devyn had light brown skin like Tobyn, the same gently freckled shoulders, and long, wavy, dark brown hair. Her sister redid her bun, taming all the fuzzy hairs with edge control and a tough-bristled brush, then slipped into a pair of ripped jeans and an off-the-shoulder green shirt that made her brown eyes seem even browner.

"Where's your roommate?" Tobyn asked.

"Spending the night with her boyfriend, but she said she might meet us at the show."

Devyn had always been curvy, but Tobyn noticed her sister's jeans sagging a little, in a way they normally didn't. "Are you like on a diet or something?" Tobyn asked.

Devyn laughed but didn't answer.

The show was dark, so Tobyn easily used her sister's ID to buy a drink from the guy bartender right after Devyn had ordered from a girl at the other end of the counter. Once they had their drinks they made their way through the crowd to stand close to the stage.

The singer they'd come to see was young and gorgeous, and her voice rose like smoke in the room. "She's so good!" Tobyn shouted.

"You should be up there!" Devyn yelled into Tobyn's ear. "She's good, but you're better!"

Tobyn grinned and nodded to the beat of the

music. Whenever Tobyn came to shows like this one, she couldn't help but imagine herself on stage. She wanted it more than anything, and the best part was, she believed deep in her bones that she would make it happen.

After a few songs, Devyn got another drink and spotted her roommate, Mae, and her tattooed boyfriend. They squeezed through the thick audience to stand right beside them.

"Hey! Glad we found you guys! My friend Jazmine's band is here, too. They're playing next!" Mae said.

When the first singer's set ended, Tobyn checked her phone. She had a text from Micah.

You up? was all it said. Tobyn knew that sometimes Micah had trouble sleeping because of her anxiety, and she wondered if her friend was lying awake missing her brother. Tobyn looked over at Devyn. She couldn't imagine losing her sister the way Micah had lost Milo.

> I am. At a show with Devyn. It's not too far from your place if you want to come.

Tobyn knew good girl Micah probably wouldn't sneak out at this hour, hop on the subway, and join them, but part of her was always hoping Micah would get a little braver.

Where is it? Micah asked. Tobyn sent the name and address of the club.

> There's a $10 cover. Are you really thinking about coming?

Micah didn't text back.

Mae's friend's band was called Maybe

Someday, and when they walked out on stage something like fire filled Tobyn's belly. The band was made up of three girls. Mae's friend Jazmine, who had short, bright red hair, was the singer.

"Hey, guys, thanks for coming out. That's Tala over there on the drums," Jazmine said. Tala had brown skin, long dreadlocks, and a wide grin. She held a drumstick in the air and waved. "This tall drink of water is Sky." Jazmine pointed to the other girl, who was long-limbed with pale skin and blond hair. She was holding a guitar. "I'm Jazz and we're Maybe Someday," Jazmine said into the mic. "We're gonna play some songs for you." The crowd screamed.

Tobyn realized that this band was the headliner. These girls, who looked like they could be her age or just a tiny bit older, were the act that most of the crowd had come to see. Tobyn grabbed Devyn's hand and pushed closer to the stage, an idea building in her head the second she heard Jazmine's unbelievably deep voice.

About halfway through Maybe Someday's set, Tobyn felt a tug on the back of her shirt. She turned around to see Micah standing there in one of her floral skirts and a denim jacket. Her boyfriend Ty was with her. "Yay!" was all Tobyn said, and Devyn tossed an arm across Micah's shoulder like she'd always belonged between them. Tobyn wished all the Flyy Girls had come to hang out. When her phone buzzed with another text, she silently hoped it was from Noelle. But it was from her girlfriend, Ava.

I can't sleep. What are you doing?

Earlier that day, Ava had stared at her phone while Tobyn told her the story about the very first time she and Devyn had snuck out to go to a show. Tobyn had only been thirteen, and sixteen-year-old Devyn knew about a fire exit the venue never locked. Devyn and her friends had been sneaking into shows for weeks and lying low in the dark, just to hear the music. Tobyn knew it was a great story because when she'd told the Flyy Girls, they'd squealed and asked her a million questions and wanted to hear the ending (when she and Devyn got chased out by bouncers) a thousand times, but Ava just said "Cool," without so much as looking up. A few minutes later, Ava showed Tobyn a comment someone had left on one of Ava's photos. Lately her girlfriend seemed more concerned with how many followers she had and the number of likes her selfies got than anything that was going on with Tobyn.

When Tobyn glanced over at Micah and Ty,

they were whispering into each other's ears and laughing. They always seemed to be so in love, and Tobyn wanted to know what that felt like almost as badly as she craved being on stage. Maybe she'd never been in love if this was what real love looked like. Tobyn wondered what it meant that she hadn't thought of Ava all night while she couldn't stop thinking about Noelle.

Instead of texting her girlfriend back, Tobyn looked Maybe Someday up on her phone. She followed the band everywhere they had an account. In the caption of their most recent post she saw something that made her heart thud harder in her chest: *We're looking to add a new member to Maybe Someday. Do you have what it takes? Stay tuned for the details!*

After the show, a drunk Devyn was singing loudly as they walked into the chilly March weather. Ty laughed and said, "Shhhh."

Tobyn showed her friends and her sister the post calling for a new band member and asked what they all thought. "I need to be in that band," Tobyn told them.

Ty said, "Better stay tuned then."

Micah said, "You'd be perfect."

"You're definitely good enough, boo," Devyn agreed. "But what about school? You know Mom is gonna be on you about that."

Micah nodded. "Didn't she already pressure you into applying to a few places?"

She'd tried to. But Tobyn had never planned on going to college for real. And now that she'd seen Maybe Someday and had imagined how her high, clear soprano would be a perfect complement to Jazmine's sultry alto, she knew exactly what she had to do.

The Harlem High Notes performed pretty regularly both in and outside of school. The day after the Maybe Someday show, Tobyn was running late to an a cappella showcase they were participating in in Midtown. She'd been so engrossed in the new song she was writing on the way that she accidentally missed her stop. And when she rushed out of the train station and into the convention center, Tobyn had no idea where she was supposed to be.

She pulled out her phone to text one of the girls in her group, but before she could hit send, she felt a warm hand on her shoulder.

"You're late," Devyn said. "I've been here for like thirty minutes waiting for you. The rest of your group is up here. Let's go!"

"I didn't even know you were coming!" Tobyn said to her sister. At first, Devyn came to all of her a cappella shows, but lately her sister had missed more shows than she'd made it out to see, even after promising to be there.

Devyn had been the one who convinced Tobyn to try out after her teacher, Mr. Bronwen, told her he was starting a new a cappella group. "You'll get so much practice and exposure," Devyn had said when Tobyn mentioned the auditions at the beginning of the school year.

"But it's a big-time commitment," Tobyn said. "It's senior year. I kinda want to chill."

"It'll be worth it. Plus, you'll meet people who love singing as much as you do. My first band was made up of people I got to know right before I graduated. Give it a chance."

So Tobyn had auditioned. When she was offered a spot, she took it even though the twice-a-week practices and constant performances made her already busy schedule even busier.

Now, the sisters stepped into a big room

where lots of other groups were warming up their voices. Devyn pointed to where the Harlem High Notes were, and Tobyn kissed Devyn's cheek before heading over to them.

"Sorry I'm late," she said. Mr. Bronwen seemed more disappointed than upset. "I'm just glad you made it," he said. "We're practicing 'Pretty Hurts,' tweaking the arrangement slightly. I almost gave away your solo."

Tabitha, a girl in the group who had seemed jealous of how often Tobyn was picked for solos, glared in Tobyn's direction. "Nice of you to join us," she snapped.

Tobyn didn't respond.

On stage, Tobyn's voice soared. Devyn watched from the front row, and it meant the world to Tobyn to have her sister there. It made her remember the way Devyn would put her hand on Tobyn's diaphragm and tell her to sing "from here." Tobyn imagined her sister's hand against her belly, and forced her voice to be bigger, stronger than it already was. Tobyn wanted to make Devyn proud.

When they finished, Devyn was the first one out of her seat, and after, she gave her sister a bouquet of wildflowers.

"Keep singing, little sis," Devyn said as she handed them over, her eyes pooling with tears. In her whole life, Tobyn had only seen her sister cry twice. "Dev, what's going on? Are you okay?" Her sister nodded, but tears still spilled over. Alarmed, Tobyn quickly wrapped Devyn in a hug.

"I promise I'll never stop," Tobyn whispered.

3

"Breakfast is almost ready," Tobyn said as her mom walked in Monday morning.

Tobyn's mom, Sabrina Wolfe, worked the overnight shift at a swanky boutique hotel downtown. She slept most of the day while Tobyn was at school and left for her shift after dinner, so if Tobyn had a cappella rehearsal or hung out with the girls after school, sometimes breakfast was the only meal the two of them had together. Every day, before her mom got home, Tobyn would brew coffee for herself, and make her mom a cup of herbal tea. Then they'd eat together in their sun-dipped kitchen before Tobyn got dressed for school and her mom got ready for bed.

That day, Tobyn had made them fried egg BLTs. Her mom liked hers with ketchup, so Tobyn set out the bottle as her mom dropped her keys into the tray by the door and slipped out of her high heels.

"You're a saint," her mother whispered as she sat down, touched her forehead, chest, and each shoulder in prayer before taking a bite. Tobyn grinned and sat across from her.

"How was work?" Tobyn asked.

"Not too bad. Only had one annoying guest who insisted her towels were dirty and asked us to replace them three different times."

"Rich people are the worst," Tobyn said.

Her mother smiled. "What have you been up to lately?"

"Had an a cappella show, and I saw Devyn a couple times," Tobyn said. "She seems . . . I don't know. Different. Weirdly forgetful and kinda sad. It looks like she's losing weight, too."

Tobyn's mom didn't say anything. She just took another bite of her sandwich. They talked about other things—school and the weather and Ava. Tobyn hadn't told her mom about what had happened with Noelle or the feelings that seemed to be blossoming inside her. When they were almost done with breakfast, Tobyn swallowed the last sip of her coffee and noticed her mom staring at her wrist. Sabrina said, "Where'd you get that bracelet?"

"Oh, Dev gave it to me. Isn't it cute?"

Her mother cupped her mug of tea with both hands. "Maybe you should think about spending a little less time at your sister's place."

"Have you been saying that to Devyn?"

Tobyn asked. But her mother didn't answer.

"Your sister has her own life now, you know? And so do you. I know you two used to be close, and maybe you will be again, but right now she needs to focus on getting her life together, and you should be more focused on school and getting into college. I mean, next year you might not even be in New York."

Tobyn *didn't* plan on being in New York next year, but not for the reasons her mom expected. Sabrina thought her daughter might be going off to college, while Tobyn had grand plans to be touring either solo or with a band.

"Right. Which is all the more reason why I should spend time with her now. And what do you mean she needs to get her life together? Why are you always so down on Devyn?"

"Just . . . stay focused okay? Get the grades you need and figure out where you're going to enroll next year. I don't want your sister to be a distraction."

✿✿✿

At school, before first bell, Tobyn and Micah told the girls about the Maybe Someday show.

"I can't believe goody-two-shoes Micah actually snuck out!" Lux said. She grabbed Micah's shoulders and shook her like she was proud.

"It was an all-girl band?" Noelle asked, and when Micah nodded, Noelle said, "That's so cool."

"Who do they sound like?" Lux asked.

"Like my freaking future," Tobyn replied, and they all laughed. "I can imagine the way me and Jazz could harmonize. It would be like magic."

"Did they post the details yet?" Lux asked.

"No, but I've been checking. I'm sure lots of

people are going to enter."

"Won't matter," Noelle said kind of quietly. "No one stands a chance if your voice is in the running."

Tobyn glanced at Noelle and felt a flutter in the pit of her stomach, but she didn't know if it was from Noelle's quiet compliment, or the way her friend's curls were falling so gorgeously over her shoulders. Ever since their kiss, she tried not to look at Noelle for too long, but Tobyn couldn't turn her eyes away right then. Noelle blushed and looked down.

"That was actually nice of you to say, Noelle," Micah said, like she was surprised. And Lux laughed.

"What was nice?" Ava asked. Tobyn kissed her girlfriend on the cheek and told her about Maybe Someday. Tobyn didn't look in Noelle's direction for the rest of lunch, but she wondered if Ava, who was looking at her phone again, would have even noticed if she did.

That evening, the Flyy Girls gathered on Micah's rooftop. As they got settled, Noelle explained how Ms. Porter, the orchestra teacher, was helping her prepare for the audition she had coming up with the Manhattan School of Music. Tobyn was scrolling through her feed when a new post from Maybe Someday made her freeze.

Beneath a photo of the band the caption read, *Wanna sing with Maybe Someday? Record a video of you singing one of our songs and share it with the hashtag #SingWithMaybeSomeday by midnight Friday. We'll pick our favorite ten performers to come and audition with us in person.* The image featured a photoshopped silhouette of a fourth member.

"Yes!" Tobyn shouted.

"What just happened?" Noelle asked.

"Maybe Someday wants people who want to join the band to post a video of their singing. They're going to pick their favorites for in-person auditions."

"Oh snaps," Lux said.

"Sounds like trying to get into college," Noelle joked.

Tobyn nodded. "Maybe you and Ms. Porter can give me some pointers on how to audition if I make it that far."

"That's so exciting!" Micah said. "Are you just going to post a video you already have?"

"No," Tobyn answered. "I have an idea. But Lux, I'll need your help."

After Tobyn told them her plan, and that she wanted to record the video that Friday, Noelle grinned and said, "I'm definitely coming." Lux agreed to help, and Micah said she'd be there, too.

Tobyn knew Ava would insist on coming once she knew about it, but she tried not to think too hard about how Noelle and Ava didn't really get along. She'd never told Ava that Noelle kissed her after the fall showcase, but it was like Ava could tell something had happened. She got extra touchy with Tobyn whenever Noelle was around, like she wanted to let Noelle know Tobyn belonged to her. Tobyn didn't like it, especially since in private Ava barely paid her any attention, but she didn't know what to do about it.

The house was empty when Tobyn got home, so she knew her mom had already left for work. Sabrina Wolfe had stuck a note to the fridge asking Tobyn to clean up, so Tobyn turned on some music and started singing and dancing around the apartment. She texted Devyn, telling her about her plan, and then she got to work. She dusted and put away the laundry that had been dropped off from the wash-n-fold delivery service they used once a month. She did the dishes and even stacked her mom's dozens of boxes of high heels more neatly in her closet. She was singing so loudly by the end of her cleaning session that her neighbor banged on the wall. "Sorry, Mrs. Pratt!" Tobyn yelled, before turning down the music and opening her song book. She jotted down some new lyrics, then checked her phone. She had a message from Ava, but nothing from Devyn. Which was weird. Devyn always texted her back right away.

Tobyn replied to Ava's text and told her about Friday. Just as Tobyn thought she would, Ava replied and said, **Can't wait!**

TEXTS FROM TOBYN TO DEVYN

MONDAY, MARCH 15, 5:27 P.M.

I have kind of a crazy idea.

Maybe Someday wants people to post a video of themselves singing to qualify for an in-person audition with them.

Two questions for you:

What song should I sing that would best show off my voice?

And can you come to 110th Street Station around 7 on Friday?

4

Over the next three days, Tobyn sang as she made breakfast for her mom, as she showered and got dressed, as she walked down the hallways at school, and whenever she hung out with the girls on Micah's rooftop. She sang in her empty apartment late at night, and of course she sang at a cappella rehearsals. On Thursday, Mr. Bronwen noticed her extra enthusiasm. "You've been practicing, huh?" he said, and she nodded. Tobyn tried and failed to ignore Tabitha's eyes on her. As rehearsal ended on Thursday, Mr. Bronwen pulled Tobyn aside.

"I'm glad to see that you've been working on our arrangements outside of rehearsals. I can definitely hear the difference. And with the citywide competition coming up at the end of the month, I've been keeping my eye out for people showing leadership and dedication to their craft for the solos. You were already on my radar, but this extra effort has really made you stand out."

Tobyn grinned and clapped, and Mr. Bronwen laughed. The prospect of having another solo was exciting, especially since it was a competition. "Thank you so much for saying that, Mr. B!"

Mr. Bronwen nodded. "Auditions for the solo parts will be the week before we compete, and while I'm pretty sure you'll be one of my first picks, I still want to see you sing that day with everyone else. Keep singing like this, and I think the Harlem High Notes have a chance at the $25,000 prize."

Tobyn's eyes grew wide. "$25,000?" she asked, and Mr. Bronwen nodded. "To go toward whatever you want to do next—music school or studio time. It's meant to keep you singing."

Tobyn ignored the immediate image of Tabitha rolling her eyes or making a rude comment if Tobyn was picked again for a solo. Instead, she thought about what she could do with the money and the promise she'd made to her sister to keep singing no matter what, and nodded.

By Friday, Tobyn felt ready and excited to make her video, but she'd kept what Mr. Bronwen had told her in the back of her mind. If things didn't work out with Maybe Someday, she needed a backup plan, and maybe helping the Harlem High Notes win the competition could be it. Mr. B said she could use the prize money for studio time, and other than joining an already successful band, recording a demo might be one of the only other ways to convince her mother that singing could be a good choice for the future. With only nine other members of the Harlem High Notes, her share of the prize money—$2,500—could pay for more than enough studio time to record something she was proud of.

As Tobyn walked to the train station that morning, she tried calling her sister. She wanted Devyn's help deciding what song she should sing, but more than that, Tobyn really wanted her sister to be there tonight, rooting for her.

But Devyn's phone didn't even ring—it went straight to voicemail. That had never happened, and Tobyn felt a stirring in her gut that wasn't nervousness about the coming performance. She sent her a text instead, trying to ignore any anxious thoughts about why her sister wasn't answering, reminding herself that Devyn had been kind of unreliable lately. Besides, Tobyn knew she needed to focus. On her grades so her mom wouldn't kill her. On improving her voice control and strength, so she could get that a cappella solo. And on tonight, because Maybe Someday could be her future.

All morning, Tobyn struggled to pay attention in her classes. And when she sat down in the Yard with her friends during lunch, she tried her best not to think about Devyn or a cappella or Maybe Someday.

Noelle opened a folder full of marked-up

sheet music, stuck her hands into her curls, and said, "This piece I'm working on is giving me so much trouble." Tobyn leaned over to see what Noelle meant, happy for the distraction.

"Lemme see that," Tobyn said. Even though Tobyn had always been a vocal-music-focused student at Augusta Savage, she'd taken piano lessons when she was younger and still played occasionally, so she knew how to read music. And she was always writing songs, though no one knew that. She hummed the piece to herself, imagining the belly-deep sounds of Noelle's cello. Sometimes she thought the cello sounded a lot like a voice, and she wished she could be as brave with her songs as Noelle always was.

"This is really beautiful, Noelle," she said. "But I think I see the problem."

"Right!?" Noelle agreed as they both pointed

to a refrain near the center of the song. Tobyn sang the notes out loud, and one part sounded a little off, like the song was falling out of key.

"What if you . . ." Tobyn took Noelle's pencil from her, erased a few notes, and made a quick change. "So now it would sound like . . ." She sang the new notes and Noelle nodded.

"Ooh, I like that. But what about this?"

Together the girls made a few more changes to Noelle's song while Lux and Micah ate their lunch and talked about the assignments they were working on. Tobyn kept snatching the pencil from Noelle and playfully arguing with her about the end of the song. "My way sounded better," Tobyn said, leaning in close to Noelle. "You know I'm right."

"No," Noelle countered. "You just *think* you are." She grabbed Tobyn's wrist and plucked the pencil from her fingers. Tobyn couldn't help but notice how soft Noelle's palm was. And that, by contrast, the tips of her fingers were warm and rough—callused from playing her instrument. She also noticed Micah and Lux had gone quiet. And Lux was even smirking, looking in their direction.

"Hey, boos, what's up?" Ava asked, seeming to appear out of nowhere. Noelle dropped Tobyn's wrist as Ava stepped over the bench of their table to sit between them.

"Nothing," Noelle said. "Tobyn was just helping me fix my song."

"Well, she is very good at stuff like that, aren't you, bae?" Ava asked. She pulled out her phone and started to scroll and double-tap.

Noelle straightened her glasses and rolled her eyes, hard.

Tobyn's throat felt dry. She nodded.

"T!"

Tobyn was standing by the stairs in the 110th Street station that evening when she heard the nickname the Flyy Girls called her. She turned to see Noelle waiting on the platform with Micah and Lux and quickly walked over to them. Noelle handed her a thermos, and when Tobyn unscrewed the top and took a sip, she tasted warm water with lemon and honey—Tobyn's favorite before-singing drink.

"For your throat," Noelle said. And Tobyn smiled at her sweetness. Noelle glanced away, but she kept talking. "So I was thinking about it, and you should pick a song with high notes that can show off your range. Especially since you said Jazz's voice is a low alto. I was just thinking about how your voice sounds with the cello and I thought . . ."

"How do you know what my voice sounds like with the cello?" Tobyn asked.

"Oh. I guess I've imagined it a lot," Noelle replied.

Tobyn stared at her and Noelle stared right back, but neither girl said anything else, and before either of them could, Lux pulled out her camera. Micah pointed out the perfect spot on the platform where she thought Tobyn could be heard but not in the way, and then Ava arrived.

"Hey. How long have you guys been here?" Ava asked.

"We all just got here," Tobyn said, pulling her eyes away from Noelle, who had imagined her singing along while she played cello; who had gotten her warm water for her voice; who had kissed her in a way she couldn't seem to forget no matter how hard she tried. Tobyn cleared her throat and smiled at her girlfriend. "Don't worry, you haven't missed anything."

"Good," Ava said. "I wanted to livestream this!"

Tobyn scanned the station looking for Devyn, but she was nowhere.

Devyn had been her inspiration for deciding to record her entry at a subway station, singing loudly so her voice echoed off the cave-like walls. She wished Devyn was there, but she couldn't wait forever. She stood in the spot Micah had suggested, in front of a pretty mosaic, and Lux lifted her camera and pressed record while Ava did the same with her phone.

Tobyn belted out a song with high notes, like Noelle had suggested, while thinking about Noelle's curly hair, her smudged glasses, the way she'd been trying so hard to be kinder– even to Ava. She thought about her sister and her mom and how much she loved them. More than anything, Tobyn thought about how badly she wanted to keep singing. She hoped she'd be singing forever.

There were delays on the 2 and 3 train lines, so the platform kept getting more and more crowded. Tobyn kept singing. She noticed a guy pull out his earbuds and turn to watch her. A woman with long black hair lifted her toddler up on her shoulders so the kid could see. A hipster in big glasses and bright red lipstick pulled out her phone and aimed it in Tobyn's direction.

Halfway through Tobyn's third song, an older couple in front of her started dancing. One by one, other people joined in until nearly everyone on the platform was part of her performance. Those who weren't dancing were recording everyone else on their phones, and when the song ended just as a train arrived, everyone applauded. So many people came up to her asking where they could find more of her music, and Tobyn didn't know what to say. She just told them about Maybe Someday and the audition and how badly she wanted it. They all wished her luck. When the girls left, they couldn't stop talking about what had happened, and even Ava told Tobyn she'd been fabulous. "Proud of you, bae," Ava said. With her friends' excitement, Ava's compliments, and the attention from the strangers on the platform, Tobyn felt warm and wanted; seen and celebrated—feelings she was always chasing.

Tobyn fell asleep early that night for the first time in months, but not before texting Devyn to tell her everything.

5

"I can't believe she didn't come!" Noelle said.

"Stop moving so much," Lux said. She was painting Noelle's nails. It was the weekend, and Lux, Noelle, Micah, and Tobyn were over at Lux's apartment, hanging out in her "glass castle" as she'd started calling it recently, having a spa day. Micah and Tobyn were wearing sheet masks Noelle had brought from Chinatown, and Lux had jade green eye gels stuck to her face.

Tobyn stood at one of the windows and looked down at all the people on the street. She just shrugged.

"Yeah, do you know where your sister was?" Micah asked.

Tobyn shrugged again. "She's been kinda weird lately."

Tobyn remembered the way things had been with Devyn before she moved out. How they would walk to the bodega together every morning before school to get three bacon, egg, and cheeses and leave one at home for their mom. How they would ride the subway together sharing a single set of earbuds. The way they were always singing together: on the fire escape outside their bedroom, on their ivy-covered stoop, in their tiny bathroom—Tobyn on the toilet, Devyn sitting on the edge of the tub—because the acoustics were so good in there. On weekends, they'd sing at a park, or in subway stations. Devyn would leave a shoebox on the ground in front of them and sometimes people would give them change or even a few dollars, and they would buy lipstick or mascara or junk food and candy. And of course, they were always sneaking into shows. Tobyn glanced at her phone on Lux's dresser, feeling nervous about her chances of being picked to audition for Maybe Someday but also missing her sister. She hadn't heard from Devyn for a few days now.

"My mom said she wants me to hang out with her less," Tobyn told her friends. "And I don't know, Dev hasn't answered my last few calls or texts. Maybe she wants that, too."

Micah immediately tried to comfort Tobyn. "I don't think that's true," she said.

But the more Tobyn thought about it, the more she realized it could be. "She hasn't really wanted to hang out as much as she did before. She came to my last a cappella concert, but she hadn't been to one in a long time. And it seemed like she'd forgotten about the Maybe Someday show until I showed up at her place. Micah, I didn't tell you this, but when I got to her apartment that night she wasn't even dressed."

Micah looked down at her hands.

"Whatever," Tobyn said, though deep in her chest her heart felt like it was breaking. "It's fine. If she's too busy with her own life to care about me, I can be busy, too."

To change the subject, Tobyn told her friends about the a cappella competition.

"You could get $2,500?" Lux said. "That's crazy."

"That should be enough to record a short demo. My cousin recorded one, and his studio time was like $100 an hour," Noelle added.

"That's perfect. Plus, Mr. B wants to give me a solo. If I get that, it would be everything."

"So which do you want more? To join Maybe Someday or to record your own demo?" Micah asked.

"I don't know. I've always wanted to sing in a band, but being in a studio would be amazing, too. Maybe I could do both—focus on Maybe Someday and, if we do well in the competition, save the money to record a demo later? I'm not sure."

"Do you even have any songs written?" Lux asked.

Tobyn said, "Not really," and left it at that, but she thought of her beat-up song book, secreted away in her backpack.

"What about college?" Noelle asked. "What about your mom?"

Tobyn shrugged. She peeled the sheet mask off her face and tossed it into Lux's trash can.

"I guess I'll have to see how much longer I

can hold her off. Is it my turn to get my nails painted yet?"

Noelle moved out of the seat in front of Lux, and Tobyn took her place. The air around the seat smelled like Noelle—sweet, like the oil Noelle put in her hair—mixed with the strong scent of the nail polish.

As Lux started painting Tobyn's nails a bright marigold—she liked her nails to be colorful since her clothes almost never were—Tobyn glanced over at her friends' manicures. Micah's nails were white with tiny pink hearts. Lux's were still unpainted—she always did her own manicure last. Tobyn noticed that Noelle's were adorned with tiny rainbows, and before she could ask, Noelle said, "So . . . I came out to my parents."

All three of the other Flyy Girls whipped their heads in Noelle's direction.

"What?" Lux said.

"When?" Micah asked.

"How did it go? What did they say? Are you okay?" Tobyn almost shouted.

Noelle laughed.

"I'm fine. I told them last night, after we left the train station. It just felt like it was time, I guess. And I just said 'I'm not straight' because I'm still figuring out exactly what I am.'"

"Holy shit," Lux said, and Tobyn jumped up and hugged Noelle. As she held her, Tobyn's throat felt tight and her eyes stung with tears. She remembered when she had told her own mother, the way Sabrina had nodded solemnly. The way Devyn had grinned and said she couldn't wait for Pride that year. How even though neither reaction was bad, the two had made Tobyn feel so many things at once.

"I'm okay," Noelle assured them. "I swear."

"My dad looked uncomfortable," Noelle said when Tobyn let her go. Her nail polish had smudged, but she didn't care. "But my mom just smiled. Pierre hugged me, and I told my Granna, too, in a letter. I actually told her first, and when she wrote back that love was beautiful no matter what it looked like, that's what gave me the guts to tell everyone else. I'm not ready to tell Năinai and Yéye yet, but I think I will soon." Noelle glanced at Tobyn. "You helped a little, too," she added in a low voice.

Tobyn's heart started pounding. She thought about the kiss after the fall showcase, about Ava, and about what it meant for Noelle to be out. It changed things, making everything more complicated. Noelle was so brave with her identity, just as she was with her music. And suddenly, Tobyn wanted Noelle to kiss her again.

TEXTS FROM TOBYN TO DEVYN

FRIDAY, MARCH 19, 8:01 A.M.

You have to come tonight.
If you don't Noelle might kill Ava.

And I want to sing with you!

FRIDAY, MARCH 19, 8:43 P.M.

I sang and everyone on the platform
was dancing and people were asking
me where they could find my music!

I was like what? I don't even
have music . . . yet! Lol

But I think the band will have to pick me after they see how much the crowd loved me.

Dev, it was amazing. I wish you had been there to see me.

Where were you?

6

As Tobyn stepped into her Black Music History class on Monday, a Harlem High Notes member named Summer walked over to her and said, "Did you post a video of yourself singing in a subway station?"

Tobyn nodded slowly. "How'd you know about that?"

"Oh my God. That video has been everywhere, and other girls from a cappella said it was you and I didn't believe them."

"Wait, what?"

Summer took out her phone, pulled up her

messages, and held it up for Tobyn to see. On screen, she was singing on a crowded platform as people danced around her. The view count caught Tobyn's eye and she gasped.

"You went viral, girl," Summer said.

"Over 100,000 views," Tobyn announced to the girls that afternoon on Micah's roof. "Can you believe it? And it keeps rising."

The sun was slowly sinking, but its remaining light peeked over the tops of buildings and reflected off windows like bits of gold. Lux sat with her legs crossed on the concrete roof, as Micah leaned back in one of the lounge chairs. Noelle was sitting next to Tobyn, and Tobyn was trying her hardest not to think about how close she was to Noelle's pretty hands.

Just then Lux's phone dinged and she laughed. "Emmett just texted me. He said, *Is that really Tobyn?*"

"Even he's seen it?" Micah asked.

"Guess so."

"Oh my God," Noelle said a few minutes later. She was looking at her phone now, too. "#MaybeTobyn is trending."

"WHAT?" Tobyn said.

"Probably because you kept talking about the band when people asked about your music?" Lux suggested. "Didn't you tell a bunch of people about how Maybe Someday was trying to find their new member?"

Tobyn covered her face and nodded. She was smiling so hard her cheeks ached. "This is crazy," she said.

Tobyn checked Maybe Someday's account, but they hadn't posted anything new. She wondered if going viral would help or hurt her chances.

"Do you think Jazz has seen it?" Micah asked. "Doesn't your sister's roommate know her? Ask Devyn if Mae has heard anything!"

Tobyn pulled out her phone to text her sister. But if Devyn didn't answer her this time, she was done. This was too important for Devyn to ignore.

In a cappella rehearsal the next day, the video was all anyone was talking about. But the group was intensely divided.

Summer and a few of the other girls were in awe and so excited for Tobyn. "They have to pick you to audition after this!" Summer said. "There's no way you won't make the top ten," another girl, Yara, agreed. "I actually saw Ava's livestream before I saw the original video you posted, Tobyn. She got almost as many views as you!" a girl named Lianne said loudly.

And then, there was the other half of the Harlem High Notes. A girl named Rose said, "What if they think you staged it? I mean, *I* don't think that, but it does look pretty fake." Tabitha jumped in right away, like she'd been waiting for someone to say something like that. "Right? All those people just randomly on the platform? And dancing just because *you're* singing?" Tabitha shrugged, and a couple of the girls around her nodded. "Real New Yorkers don't pay attention to street performers like that."

"There was a delay," Tobyn started to explain, but Tabitha cut her off. "The trains—"

"You think you're some kind of It Girl. But you're really just shit, girl," Tabitha said. Rose and a few other girls laughed.

When Mr. Bronwen came into the room to start rehearsal, all chatter stopped. And though Tobyn knew Tabitha was just jealous, she worried she might have a point. Did what happened in the station look staged? Would Maybe Someday think she cheated?

That night, Tobyn was stressed about Maybe Someday, anxious about a cappella, and confused and angry about Devyn not texting or calling her back. She tried calling Ava, but her girlfriend texted that she was busy without picking up, and said she'd call her later. Tobyn started to text her friends' group chat next, but quickly realized the only person she really wanted to talk to was Noelle.

TEXTS FROM TOBYN TO NOELLE

TUESDAY, MARCH 23, 10:19 P.M.

Hey

Heyyy

I'm stressed.

School? Your mom?
The thing with the band?

All-a-dat

LOL

You always have so much going on.
How do you deal?

Talking to my Granna helps. Cello helps.

Beating Pierre at video games REALLY helps.

That's about it.

Yeah.

Singing usually helps, but without anyone to talk to it's all a lot.

Can you talk to Ava?

Ava just wants to post photos and get likes.

When was the last time she even posted a picture with you?

Now that you mention it, it's been a while.

If you were my girl, I'd be posting pictures of you all the time.

Sorry.

If that was like too much or whatever.

It wasn't.

I'm just still getting used to "Nice Noelle."

Don't get too comfortable.

Lol

Your sister still not writing back?

Nope.

Well, you know you can always talk to me.

At breakfast later that week, Tobyn decided to tell her mom about Maybe Someday. They were eating chocolate chip pancakes that were topped with strawberries and whipped cream. It was one of her mom's favorite things to have for breakfast, and Tobyn hoped it would make her mother more willing to listen.

"So Mom," Tobyn started slowly. "There's this band . . ." She always felt a little exposed when she talked to her mom about music. In some ways talking about music was more frightening than coming out had been—singing was just as much a part of her identity as being a girl who loved girls was. Music would always be a part of her, and it scared her that it was something her mother could say was unimportant.

"A band?" her mother asked.

"Yes. And I want to join it. They're called Maybe Someday, and they're really good." Tobyn picked up her phone and navigated to their page. She hit play on a video of one of their best songs, and her mom watched it closely.

"Wow," Sabrina said. "They have a lot of followers. And is that number how many views this video has gotten?" Tobyn nodded. Before her nerves got the best of her, she pulled up her own video singing the same song.

"Wait," her mother said. She looked up at Tobyn and then back down at the video. "Is that . . . you?"

Tobyn nodded again. "Maybe Someday

is running this . . . contest to find a new band member. This is the video I posted to enter, and yeah, it's getting a lot of attention. I think this could be a big deal for me. I wanted you to know and to see this—that I'm good."

Her mom put down her fork. "So you think just because a few thousand people on the Internet liked some video of yours, I'm going to let you throw away your future?"

Tobyn looked from the phone to her mom's face. "Why do you think singing is throwing away my future? And if you thought that all along, why'd you enroll me in a performance arts high school?"

Her mother picked up her cup of tea. "I sent you to that school because in addition to having the arts, Augusta Savage has excellent academics. I was trying to balance your interests with your needs. And while I think you're talented and I admire your confidence, baby, I think you need to be more realistic here. Bands are . . . complicated. Music is fine as something you do on the side, or for fun, but I know it's not a smart career choice. You should focus on getting into a good college. Remind me, where have you applied so far?"

Tobyn lied. She made up a list of a few schools on the spot. The truth was, she'd only even *thought* about applying to one: the Manhattan School of Music, and only because Noelle had applied there.

"I'm still sure I want to sing, though, not go to school right after graduation. I can always go to college, but it's my dream to make music. Maybe Someday could be a real chance to do that," Tobyn told her mother.

"This isn't a debate, Tobyn Marie. I mean, you see what's happened with your sister.

Her band isn't even together anymore!"

"Wait." Tobyn froze. "What?"

"You spend all that time with Devyn and you didn't know?" Sabrina asked.

Tobyn felt embarrassed. She swallowed hard and looked down at her now soggy pancakes.

"No," Tobyn said quietly.

Her mother sighed.

"Your sister asked if she could move back in a couple of months ago because the band had broken up. I asked her if she was planning on getting a real job. She said no, that music was her life. So *I* said no, because here in the real world, we have to pay rent and buy groceries."

"Wait," Tobyn said again. "She asked you to move back in?"

"Yep."

"Well, Mom," Tobyn said, "what if she asked you that because she was worried she wouldn't be able to pay *her* rent?"

"I'm sure that *is* why she asked me," Sabrina said. "But I told her the same thing I'm telling you. That music shouldn't be your Plan A. The industry is too unpredictable. And you better uncross those arms and remember who you're talking to."

Tobyn hadn't even realized she'd done that. She dropped her hands into her lap and clenched her fists.

"Did you know I haven't seen or heard from her in almost a week?" Tobyn asked, feeling guilty about how angry she'd been about the missed calls and texts. "What if something's wrong? What if she really needed your help?"

Her mother waved her hand in the air like she was swatting away Tobyn's words. "That's just typical Devyn. She's fine."

"How are you so sure? What if she isn't?

What if she's hurt or in danger?" Tobyn asked, her guilt changing to fear more quickly than she expected. Her eyes blurred with tears.

"Honey," her mother said. "Calm down. It's okay." Sabrina looked at her plate, then up at the ceiling, then back at her daughter. She gently placed her fingers over Tobyn's hand, which was resting on the table beside her. "I spoke to your sister yesterday. She's fine, I swear. Look, just tell me more about this band?"

"Yesterday?" Tobyn asked. She moved her hand away from her mother's.

"She calls me every week to check in. I asked that she start doing that so I wouldn't worry."

"So wait. She *has* been ignoring me on purpose?" Tobyn was so confused.

"Oh honey. I know you love the spotlight. And apparently, it loves you back. But everything isn't always about you."

That afternoon, Mr. Bronwen held solo auditions for the upcoming competition, which would happen the following week. The High Notes had been practicing their set list, rotating different soloists in and out to get a feel for whose voice best fit the needs of each arrangement. Now was Tobyn's moment of truth, and as she stepped to the front of the music room to take her turn at the mic, she couldn't help but overhear the other girls in the group whispering about the video again.

"I bet she thinks she has this in the bag, just

because she's Internet famous."

"Oh my God, don't be such a hater."

"Well, she's always thought she was better than the rest of us."

"Yeah, and the video made it worse."

"Maybe Mr. B won't choose her since she's been picked for a lot of solos this year . . ."

"Because she's talented. Duh."

"Will you all shut up and let her sing?"

Tobyn tried to block them all out, but when she'd stopped thinking about the whispers, thoughts of her sister filled her head. She imagined Devyn looking down at her phone and hitting ignore when she saw Tobyn's name; Devyn deleting her texts, leaving them unanswered. She imagined that she and her sister would never get back to the relationship they had before, and she was angry at herself for wanting it so badly. She tried to tell herself that maybe her sister was dealing with a lot. But Devyn's decision to cut Tobyn out of her life still hurt. And while she felt sad, Tobyn also felt determined to prove she wasn't someone who could be ignored for long.

Tobyn sang like her sister was in the room—like she needed to show Devyn she was worth caring about. She sang like this song, this one moment, could convince her mother that pursuing a music career wasn't a waste of time. She sang like she would if she got the chance to perform in front of Maybe Someday, or like she was back on that subway platform. She closed her eyes and sang as well as she could, and when she finished her song and opened her eyes, Mr. Bronwen was smiling and the other girls were no longer whispering. Tobyn saw Ava in the back of the room with her phone lifted like she was taking a photo of her.

She smiled, touched that her girlfriend had remembered the auditions and that she'd come.

"That was gorgeous, Tobyn," Mr. Bronwen said. He smiled widely at her and wrote something down on the clipboard he had in hand. From where Tobyn stood, it looked more like a check mark than an X, but she wouldn't know for sure until tomorrow.

"Thank you."

"Ava posted a video of your solo audition," Lux said as soon as Tobyn sat down at their lunch table.

"What? How? Auditions *just* ended."

Lux handed her phone to Tobyn. On the screen Tobyn saw herself in the music room, and as she scrolled quickly through a few more of Ava's recent posts, she saw that there were other videos of her, and in all of them she was singing.

"This is . . . so weird," Tobyn said. "Why is she suddenly posting all these videos of me?"

"Probably to get more followers," Noelle muttered without looking away from the oxtail stew she'd brought for lunch. She shielded her mouth with the back of her hand and kept chewing and talking. "You are kinda Internet famous, and—no shade—but you know how obsessed she is with attention."

Micah giggled. Lux laughed, too, choking on her milk a little. "It's why you're so perfect for each other," Lux said, still laughing. "And now that I think about it, probably why you fight so much. You make everything about you, and so does she."

"Ouch," Tobyn said, because even though

Lux hadn't said it in a mean way, it still stung.

Tobyn knew Lux was right, and she felt embarrassment rise in her chest like heat. She'd thought Ava had come to surprise *her*, but Ava had really come for herself.

Under normal circumstances Tobyn wouldn't mind the posted videos—as Lux had pointed out, she loved attention, too, after all— but before the video on the subway platform went viral, Ava hadn't posted a single photo of Tobyn in months. Between this and Ava getting upset when she and Noelle spent any time together, it was starting to feel like Ava only cared about Tobyn if someone else was paying attention to her. It reminded Tobyn of Devyn's silence and her mother's distance. It reminded her how heartbreaking it was to have the world watching her, while being ignored by the people she loved most.

"Well, I'm not going to just let her use me like this," Tobyn said. But before she stood up to go find Ava and confront her, a notification popped up on her phone. Tobyn froze and stared.

"What?" Micah asked. "What happened?"

"I just got a DM," Tobyn replied. "From Maybe Someday."

"Well, open it!" Noelle said a little too loudly.

"I don't think my fingers are working right now."

"They just posted something new on their page, too," Lux said.

Tobyn looked up, and Lux started reading it out loud.

"Okay, people! If you entered a video into the #SingWithMaybeSomeday competition, we've selected who will have an opportunity to audition. By the end of today, if you've been selected to audition, we will DM you a link to

download backstage passes to our upcoming

concert this weekend. Auditions will take place

before the show."

"Is it a backstage pass?" Noelle was practically yelling now.

"If you're not going to open it," Lux said, leaning across the lunch table and grabbing for Tobyn's phone, "I will."

Tobyn's fingers were slack, and Lux took the phone from her easily. Her three friends crowded around as Lux opened the message.

"There's a link!" Micah said.

"It's the passes!" Noelle screamed.

Lux turned the phone so Tobyn could see, and on screen she saw the words BACKSTAGE PASS above Maybe Someday's logo: a yellow, half-risen sun.

"Dude," Lux said, handing the phone back to Tobyn. "You get to audition for Maybe Someday."

TEXTS FROM TOBYN TO AVA

THURSDAY, MARCH 25, 8:13 P.M.

Hey do you have a sec?

There was something I wanted to talk to you about.

Sure.

Wait.

OMG.

Did you get the Maybe Someday audition???

I don't know yet.

What do you mean you don't know!

They said they'd DM everyone by the end of today.

Since when do you follow Maybe Someday?

Uhhhh since you entered their competition, duh.

Have you checked your DMs?

Not yet.

Well check!

Okay. But I wanted to talk to you about something else.

We can't talk about ANYTHING until you see if you have those backstage passes.

I could make a video of the whole thing: getting ready, going to the show, your audition!

Oh! Maybe we could even just go live the whole time.

Ava, I don't think I want to do that.

Did you check yet?

I didn't get the passes.

Oh.

Really?

What a bummer.

Can we talk though?

Sure. But let's do it tomorrow.
I'm exhausted.

Night boo. <3

TEXTS FROM TOBYN TO NOELLE

I'm freaking out.

LOL. Why??

This is like . . . the closest I've ever gotten to anything I've ever wanted this badly.

Ah.

And like, I can't tell my mom.

I just lied about it to Ava.

And I don't even have Devyn to celebrate with.

Well you know we're proud of you.

And hype as hell, too.

Lol. Yeah, I know. You guys are the best.

I was wondering . . .

Yeah?

Would you want to take my other backstage pass?

I have two and I'm sure Micah and Lux are gonna come to the show . . .

But they'll probably bring their boyfriends.

I . . . don't want to be backstage alone.

T. Are you serious?

I would freaking love to!!

9

Tobyn's hands were shaking while she got ready for the Maybe Someday audition and concert that Saturday night.

"Give me that," Lux said, taking the liquid liner Tobyn had been attempting to apply and swiping two quick, even lines across her friend's eyelids.

"Everything will be fine," Micah said. She was wearing a short skirt and a denim jacket, and Lux had on tight skinny jeans and a blazer. Tobyn was trying very hard not to look at Noelle's cut-offs and fishnet stockings, or the bra strap that was showing every time her T-shirt slipped off her shoulder. Tobyn stared down at her own outfit, all black everything as usual, and tried to relax.

"When I'm feeling anxious," Micah continued, "I do this breathing exercise I learned in therapy." Micah walked Tobyn through it and she felt a bit better until she spotted a photo of her and Devyn in the corner of her room. It felt wrong to be doing something this big without her sister, who had taught her to sing, who had been her biggest inspiration and best cheerleader. *But Devyn is still ignoring you,* Tobyn reminded herself. *She's living her life without you, and you got this audition without her.* Tobyn shook her head to clear the thoughts of her sister that kept slipping in.

By the time Lux had finished her makeup, with Noelle cracking jokes in the background and Micah being kind and supportive, Tobyn felt ready.

"Thank you for being here," she said, looking around at each of her friends.

"Duh," they all said back at once.

Tobyn's mom was just waking up and heading to the shower when the girls were leaving.

"Where you all off to?" Sabrina asked.

"Remember that band I told you about?" Tobyn answered.

Her mother nodded and crossed her arms.

"They liked my video. I got picked. We're going to my audition now."

"Tobyn, we talked about this," Sabrina said.

Tobyn tried her best to keep an even tone. But the tiniest bit of attitude slipped out. "No, Mom, *you* talked. And it seems like you didn't really listen."

"As long as you live under my roof—"

Tobyn sighed. "Mommy. I don't want to argue with you. I need you to understand how badly I want this. But if you can't . . ." Tobyn looked at her mother and she may have been imagining it, but she thought she saw Sabrina's eyes soften the tiniest bit.

"We have to go," Tobyn said. "Can we talk about it more later?"

Sabrina looked at Lux, Noelle, and Micah, who all smiled awkwardly.

"Fine," she said.

Right before Tobyn shut the door behind her, she heard her mother add, "Good luck."

At the show, Noelle and Tobyn were given passes to wear around their necks as soon as

Tobyn gave her name to the bouncer. Micah and Lux had said to look for them in the back where they were meeting Emmett and Ty, and they all promised to find each other as soon as they could. Noelle bounced with excitement, but Tobyn felt calm until they were guided to the green room where a few other auditioning singers were hanging out. Tobyn knew this was a real chance to make her dream come true, and seeing the other girls made the stakes feel higher and more real than they ever had before.

"I wish I had looked at some of the other girls' videos," Tobyn whispered to Noelle. "You know, just to size up the competition."

"It's probably better that you didn't," Noelle whispered back. "Besides, you're so good. Your video went viral! You don't need to compare yourself to anyone."

Tobyn felt Noelle's long, rough fingers lace through her own. Her friend quickly squeezed her hand and let go. Tobyn wished Noelle had held on a little longer.

Moments later, the door to the green room creaked open a crack, and then there they were—all three members of Maybe Someday.

"I'm so glad you all could make it out!" Jazz said right away. "I'm Jazz, and this is Tala and Sky. We just wanted to swing by and tell you all in person how dope your voices are. Feel free to hang out, eat some food, drink some water, and our manager will be grabbing you all one at a time to audition."

Tobyn swallowed hard.

As soon as the door closed, one of the girls standing in the far corner of the room walked up to Tobyn. "So you're the one who went viral, huh?" she said.

Tobyn felt a little shocked by how forward the girl was, but she nodded and then looked at Noelle.

"That video looked completely fake," another one of the girls said. "Staged."

"Yeah," said a third. "I mean, I just sang the song in my bedroom. Livy," she continued, pointing to a fourth girl in the room, "sang it on the roof of her apartment building. Jess sang it in her school's parking lot."

"What's your point?" Noelle asked.

"The point is," the first girl said, "that if you faked all those people dancing and applauding, it's pretty unfair that you're here with the rest of us."

"She didn't fake it," Noelle said simply. "I was there."

"Whatever," the girl called Livy said. "You can't fake anything now."

Tobyn felt her chest tighten, but she also felt like the girls' words were a challenge.

"Not that I have anything to prove to you," Tobyn said. "But I deserve to be here."

And a second later, she started singing.

She closed her eyes and raised her voice and sang like she meant it. But before she was even halfway through the first verse of the song, she heard laughter.

Tobyn opened her eyes to see one of the girls laughing at her. Tobyn stopped singing, her throat tightening in an unfamiliar way. "Oh honey," was all the girl said. And when that girl started singing, picking up the same song where Tobyn had left off, Tobyn felt her face go hot.

This girl could *really* sing. Tobyn rarely questioned her own talent, but maybe she was more out of her league than she thought. When the manager opened the door to call for the first person to follow her to the audition room, she said Tobyn's name.

Tobyn and Noelle followed her down the narrow hallway and into a room where Jazz, Tala, and Sky were seated. The manager said, "This is Tobyn Wolfe," and told Noelle she'd have to wait in the hallway. Noelle gave Tobyn's shoulder a quick squeeze and left her standing there in front of the band.

"Hi, Tobyn," Jazz said. "Thanks so much for entering our competition. Your video stood out to us so much, and not only because it got so many views." She paused to smile. "We really loved how interactive you were with the audience on the subway platform. And of course, we loved your voice."

Tobyn was frozen. She didn't say anything and she couldn't move. She couldn't even smile. This had never happened to her, but all she could think about was what the girls had said, and how strong their voices must be if the one who started singing sounded anything like how the rest of them might sound.

"Okay," Tala said. "What are you going to sing for us today?"

Tobyn just stared.

"Are you alright?" Sky asked. And Tobyn could feel her throat tightening like it had in the green room. Her chest felt like it was collapsing.

"Can I . . . have a minute?" she squeaked. Jazz looked at Tala and Tala looked at Sky, and then all three of them nodded.

Tobyn stepped into the hallway, fighting back tears. She didn't say a word to Noelle, just ran down the hall past crew members dressed in black and shoved her way into what she thought was a bathroom. She could hear

Noelle's voice and footsteps close behind her.

It wasn't a bathroom. It was a little broom closet and it was dark and close. So when Noelle followed her inside, they stood with only a few inches between them. Tobyn started to cry.

"What happened?" Noelle said.

"I completely froze," Tobyn told her. "I don't know why I freaked out like that. Singing has always come so easily to me. But I let those girls get to me. I don't know why this is so hard."

"You have a lot going on," Noelle told her. "Everything with Ava and your mom, and you still don't know why your sister is ignoring your messages, and the High Notes? I mean, there's a ton on your plate, T. Don't be so hard on yourself. You can still go back in there and own the audition. There's still a chance to make it right."

Tobyn let Noelle pull her hands away from her wet face. "You got this," Noelle said. "Don't let those dumbass, jealous girls take this away from you."

Tobyn laughed a little and nodded. Noelle still looked so pretty, even in the dark. Tobyn stepped forward, and before she could second guess what she was doing, she kissed Noelle like she'd wanted to for so long.

Noelle kissed her back. It was quiet except for the sounds of people walking past their little hiding spot. Noelle pulled away first, and asked, "What's up with you and Ava?" And Tobyn shrugged, because she didn't know what to say.

Being with Ava still felt safer than trying to be more than friends with Noelle. *But maybe,* Tobyn thought, *it would be worth the risk.*

"We should probably get you back in there,"

Noelle said quietly, and Tobyn worried Noelle was mad at her. But when they stepped out of the closet, Noelle reached out for Tobyn's hand and held it tight.

"I forgot something in the green room," Noelle said. "I'll meet you back right here when you're done with your audition." Tobyn nodded, and Noelle squeezed her hand one more time before they parted ways.

Back in the audition room, Tobyn stepped forward and sang with everything she had. This time, Jazz, Tala, and Sky smiled, and no one interrupted her at all.

Later, when Noelle and Tobyn found their friends inside the venue, Tobyn told them that her audition had gone well. Maybe Someday lit up the stage, and Tobyn could still see herself up there with them, a phantom version of herself she couldn't seem to unimagine.

Near the end of the show, when Tobyn heard the opening notes of her favorite song of theirs, Noelle grabbed her hand and pulled her through the crowd so they could get closer to the front.

"What did you forget in the green room?" Tobyn asked Noelle when they were right up against the stage. The song had just ended but it was still loud. Noelle said, "What?"

Tobyn got closer to her and asked again right up against Noelle's ear. "What did you have to go back to the green room for?"

Lux was suddenly behind them, and so were Micah and Emmett and Ty.

"She didn't forget anything in the green room," Lux said, laughing. "She made that girl who was giving you hell cry."

"You didn't," Tobyn said. And Noelle just shrugged.

"Are you surprised?" Micah asked. And Tobyn was filled with a warm fuzzy feeling in her belly.

She tossed her arm across Noelle's shoulders and kissed her on the cheek in the same moment that she felt her phone buzz in her pocket. When she pulled it out she saw a text from Ava.

No backstage passes, huh?

Tobyn was still wearing her pass around her neck, and so was Noelle. She spun around and squinted at the crowd, but she didn't see Ava anywhere.

At school on Monday, Ava was waiting by Tobyn's locker for her, arms crossed.

"So you *did* get the audition and the passes?" Ava asked. Tobyn bit her bottom lip and nodded. There was no point in lying now.

"Someone was doing a live video from the show and I saw Noelle, and I thought that was you with her, right by the stage. I could tell you were both wearing the passes. Why did you lie?"

Tobyn sighed. "I don't know, Ava. Things have been weird with us lately."

"Weird how?"

"I don't know. You don't really listen when I'm talking to you. We haven't been on a date in forever. And why are you posting all those videos of me?"

"Oh please," Ava said. "You know you love it."

"You love it, too!" Tobyn shot back. "All those people commenting and liking and following you. And it would be different if you were doing it for me or if you ever even acted like you believed in me. But I haven't felt . . . I don't know. Supported by you in a long time."

Ava rolled her eyes. "I am nothing but supportive. But all you do is lie."

Tobyn shook her head and said, "That's not true. Look, I didn't want you to livestream the whole thing or take a million videos. I wouldn't have minded you being there, if you were there for *me*, not for you. So I lied this one time because I didn't want you to be mad that I wanted to go to the audition with my girls."

"Well mission definitely *not* accomplished. I knew something was going on with you and Noelle. Do you like her? You've had weird energy with her for months," Ava said.

Tobyn took a deep breath. She didn't know why she was even staying with Ava when it was so clear they weren't right for each other anymore. Maybe she'd just gotten used to her. Maybe Ava felt the same way. But it didn't matter what Ava felt because, in that moment, Tobyn decided to tell her the truth.

"Noelle kissed me after the fall showcase. And told me she had feelings for me. But I was still figuring out how I felt about her. And you."

"She *kissed* you?" Ava shouted. She looked hurt and pissed. "I should kick her ass."

Tobyn couldn't stop the smirk that slipped onto her face. In a fight between Ava and

Noelle, it would be no contest. Noelle would knock Ava out in seconds.

"I . . . that's a bad idea," Tobyn said. "Look, Ava. I guess what I'm trying to say is—"

"Yeah, we're done," Ava said before Tobyn could. "And let the record show that *I* broke up with *you*."

Tobyn expected to feel sadder than she did about breaking up with Ava, but she mostly just felt free. The rest of the day passed quickly—classes seemed more interesting, her friends funnier than before, and Noelle seemed even prettier. At lunch, she announced that she and Ava had broken up, and the rest of the Flyy Girls applauded while Tobyn bowed.

"So now that Ava's gone," Micah asked as

soon as Noelle left the lunch table to practice cello, "what's up with you and Noelle?"

Lux raised her eyebrows and leaned forward, too, eager to hear Tobyn's plan. But Tobyn didn't really have one.

"I don't want to come on too strong, you know? I mean, she just came out. But I do think about her. A lot. I don't even know if she still feels the same way about me."

"I'm pretty sure she's obsessed with you, T," Lux said.

Micah nodded and said, "And if you want her to know how you feel, just tell her. But do it in a way that shows you really care. Everyone loves a big romantic gesture."

Tobyn found out that afternoon that she'd

been picked for an a cappella solo, at the same time as her phone began lighting up with notifications. Tobyn shoved it into her pocket.

Her phone kept buzzing while Mr. Bronwen announced the final set list and soloists for the competition, and then it buzzed all through rehearsal. Tobyn got more and more excited as the hour dragged on, hoping that all the buzzing meant news from Maybe Someday about who they picked. She'd talked herself into believing that she'd been selected, and that all of Maybe Someday's fans and her friends were congratulating her. So when rehearsal finally ended and she yanked her phone out of her pocket, she was surprised to see that something else entirely was happening.

FAKE.

Soooooo fake.

I hope she gets disqualified for this.

Ew look at her hair.

Lol bald-headed freak

HoOoOowwww did they let her audition?

Even if it is fake, she doesn't even sound that good.

God. Black girls will do anything for attention.

Lmao daddy issues for sure.

Tobyn looked around, worried the other girls in a cappella would see the comments. Her heart was pounding as she read the words and even though they were coming from strangers, she felt the weight of each insult like it was a blow to her gut. She shoved her phone back into her pocket and went to grab her stuff. She needed to find her friends so they could help her figure out what was happening.

"Ava deleted all the videos she'd posted of you," Noelle said that evening. It was the golden hour, and they were on Micah's roof soaking up the last few minutes of the day's sunlight.

"Maybe that's why all the trolls have been swarming," Lux said. "Maybe, even though Ava hadn't posted the videos to help you, she was inadvertently helping you?"

"Yeah," Micah agreed. "When people were saying the subway station video was fake, other people were linking to Ava's account as proof that it wasn't. Those videos showed you singing in more raw, simple places."

"That's true," Tobyn admitted. "That's so annoying."

"You don't have anything to prove to those haters," Noelle said. "Just block them."

"There are too many. Someone did a round-up of all the videos of the girls who got picked to audition. That's probably where most people are finding your video," Micah said.

"Disable the comments?" Noelle suggested.

"Then they might just flood my DMs. I already got a couple messages there," Tobyn said.

"If you wanted to," Lux piped up, "we could record something else in a super simple setting to shut them all up."

"That could work," Noelle agreed.

"Maybe something original, so they know you're not lip syncing to a cover of a famous song?" Micah suggested.

Tobyn thought of her song book. She glanced at Noelle, a mix of excitement and nervousness swirling in her belly, and nodded.

As soon as Tobyn woke up the following Monday, she unlocked her phone and found, in the middle of a bunch of new awful messages from trolls, a DM from Maybe Someday. She'd been stalking their accounts for news about the contest, terrified that they wouldn't be able to overlook her nervousness the day of the audition, or that they'd believe the comments that were now everywhere about her video being staged or about her voice being fake.

Before opening the DM, she checked their account, but the latest posts weren't about the contest. Finally, and with shaky hands, she sat further up in bed and read their message.

Dear Tobyn,

Thank you so much for the time and effort you put into the #SingWithMaybeSomeday contest. Your video is still one of our favorite entries. Unfortunately, we've decided to go with another singer who we felt better fit our sound and whose personality seemed to mesh best with the three of us. We think you're hugely talented, and hope you'll remain a fan.

Love,
Jazz, Tala, and Sky

At the end of the message was an invitation to a secret show they were doing to welcome the newest member of the band. It was invite-only and would just be an audience of the band members' family, closest friends, biggest fans, and all of the girls who had auditioned.

As Tobyn began reading the time and location, her vision blurred, and she realized she was crying. Huge tears fell onto the screen of her phone, and she tossed her phone aside and pulled the blanket over her head, deciding she'd stay home that day. She'd sung her best, and her best wasn't good enough.

She didn't know if she was more upset with Maybe Someday for rejecting her, or more upset with herself for failing. She cried for a long time, until she remembered that today was the a cappella competition. She couldn't let the High Notes down, and she couldn't give Tabitha the pleasure of taking over her solos. Plus, with Maybe Someday off the table, she definitely needed the High Notes to win that prize money so she could afford studio time. She rolled over, wiped her eyes, and got ready.

The competition was at Lincoln Center, and a cappella groups from all over the city were competing. It was an all-day event to accommodate all the groups who had qualified. Tobyn tried her best to swallow her disappointment so that she could do well, but her voice kept cracking during warm-ups—maybe, she thought, because she'd spent so much time that morning crying. Her vocal chords were probably swollen from her sobs. At first Tobyn thought she could hide it by singing in a lower register than she normally did. But when it happened for the third time, people started to notice.

"Whew, girl," Tabitha said. "You good?"

Tobyn rolled her eyes, nostrils flaring, and tried to stay calm.

"Can I go grab some water?" Tobyn asked Mr. Bronwen.

"We have water right here," he said, pointing to the bottles of water at the back of the room.

But Tobyn could feel tears filling her eyes. "Can I go to the bathroom?" she asked instead, feeling a little desperate and trying not to think about the rejection this morning or the way her voice was failing her now. Crying more would just make matters worse.

"Okay, but make it quick," Mr. Bronwen said. "We go on in about fifteen minutes."

Tobyn ran down a long hallway, throat tight, eyes stinging. She pushed into the bathroom and bumped right into the last person she expected to see. Devyn.

"Dev?" Tobyn asked.

Devyn was standing at the sinks, her hair looking frizzy and wild. Her face was free of makeup, but her cheeks seemed rounder, her hips less pointy, and her pants less saggy than the last time Tobyn had seen her.

"Tobyn!" Devyn said. She stepped closer to her sister and reached toward her like she was expecting to do their normal dance greeting, but Tobyn stepped back, out of her reach.

"What . . . are you doing here? And where have you been? You haven't answered any of my messages or calls for almost a month!"

Devyn looked surprised. "I've . . . had a lot going on. But I marked my calendar to come to this as soon as Mom told me about it. You don't know how much I've been looking forward to seeing you do your thing."

Tobyn frowned at her sister, confused.

"Devyn. What are you talking about? Why haven't you messaged me back? Or picked up the phone? Or come over? You basically ghosted me! Your own sister! Who does that?"

"Tobes, I can explain," Devyn started. But everything was suddenly too much for Tobyn to take. Her messed-up voice, Maybe Someday's rejection, the trolls, and now Devyn standing here acting like things were normal.

"You don't just get to be in my life when it's convenient for you, Dev. You don't get to ignore me for weeks and then pop up like everything's good."

Tobyn was crying again, but through the tears that were now running down her cheeks, she noticed a bouquet of wildflowers on the edge of the sink. Devyn picked them up.

"If you don't want me to stay, I totally

understand. I just thought—"

"You just thought what, Devyn? That I was going to be happy to see you?"

Devyn laughed a humorless laugh. "Yeah, I guess so."

"Well, I'm not. You're such a flake. I can't count on you for anything."

Devyn handed Tobyn the flowers with lowered eyes. "Good luck out there," Devyn said. "I know you'll be great."

Devyn left Tobyn standing there, wildflowers in hand. Tobyn went into a stall and balled up toilet tissue and used it to dry her eyes. She splashed water over her cheeks to try to cool her face down. She was still mad, but she pulled out her phone and texted Devyn.

If you're not gone yet, let's talk after.

Devyn didn't text back.

On stage, Tobyn was terrified her voice would break. But after she'd left the bathroom, she'd bought some tea with honey from the concession stand and sipped it slowly and carefully. She'd cleared her head of everything that was upsetting her and focused on the Harlem High Notes' setlist—all songs she knew by heart. She sang low and high, and her voice only wavered the tiniest bit on the highest notes. It wasn't the best she'd ever performed, but when their set ended and they bowed to wild applause, Tobyn felt proud.

As soon as she had a free moment, Tobyn searched the building for her sister. She even went outside and looked around the huge fountain that sat in the center of the complex.

But she didn't find her anywhere.

After a long day full of singing and listening to the other groups perform, they all gathered to hear the winners announced.

"No matter what happens," Mr. Bronwen said, "you girls really made me proud today. You should hold your heads high whether we walk out of here with trophies or not."

Tobyn crossed her fingers.

"Thank you all for coming out and spending the day with us. We're excited to announce the winners of this year's competition. First runner-up is Double Treble, from Haven High in the Bronx! Second runner-up is the Harlem High Notes from Augusta Savage School of the Arts! And our winner of the $25,000 prize and this year's champions are—"

Tobyn didn't hear the rest of what the announcer said because she realized that their name had already been called. "Second place?" Tobyn said, looking from one member of her singing group to the next. "We got second place?"

"Second place is worse than not placing," Tabitha said. "Being that close to winning and losing is torture."

"We were better than them!" Tobyn said to Mr. Bronwen. And Tabitha rolled her eyes and said, "*You weren't.*"

"Shut the hell up, Tabitha, would you?" Tobyn said. And everyone looked surprised.

Summer laughed, and Yara covered her mouth, and Lianne said, "Second place out of all these groups? I'll take it."

"Settle down, girls," Mr. Bronwen said. "Second place is an excellent outcome! I think you should all be proud."

Tobyn felt disappointed, and worried that Tabitha was right—that her solo wasn't as good as it could have been. But she clamped her jaw shut, convinced she'd do or say something worse if she kept talking.

She needed to find Devyn. And she needed a new plan for next year. She didn't know which to tackle first.

Tobyn made French toast for breakfast the next day—it was always Devyn's favorite. She was hoping her sister would show up at the apartment, but when the door opened, it was just her mom. Sabrina looked at Tobyn and asked right away, "Have you been crying?"

Tobyn had been crying, for most of the night.

She felt terrible for the things she'd said to her sister, for not hearing her out or giving her a chance to explain things. She hated that Devyn made her feel forgotten, but she knew taking all of that anger out on her sister wasn't right. Tobyn was upset about so many other things, and Devyn was the only target available for her to hit. So now if her sister never spoke to her again, at least she knew she deserved it.

"Devyn came to the a cappella competition yesterday," Tobyn said instead of answering her mother's question. She thought her red eyes and puffy face were answer enough. "I kinda lost it on her. And she's still not answering my calls or texts. If she's too busy to even pick up when I call, why did she come to my concert?"

Sabrina took a deep breath. "I think I should tell you something," she said. "Come, sit down. Let me get changed and then we'll talk."

TEXTS FROM TOBYN TO NOELLE

WEDNESDAY, APRIL 14, 10:51 P.M.

So turns out my sister hasn't been answering my calls because she's in rehab.

WHAT??

I know.

AND SHE DIDN'T TELL YOU??

She was embarrassed, I guess?

She couldn't use her phone there.

That's why she never texted back.

She got to use a landline once a week and she just called Mom.

I didn't even know her drinking was that bad.

WOW.

I know.

My mom knew and didn't tell me either.

Well, I mean, how's it . . . going?

I'm sorry. I don't really know what to ask.

It's okay. I think it's going good.

I mean, she came to my a cappella competition so I guess she finished the program.

She goes to like a sober living thing next I think.

Did you know she was coming?

No. And I totally flipped out on her.

Shit, boo.

Yeah.

Is Devyn going to be okay?

I don't really know.

Are you okay?

Not sure about that either.

I've been so focused on Maybe Someday and a capella that I didn't even see what was going on with her.

It was bad, Ellie. The things I said.

I don't know if she will forgive me.

If you want to go see her, I'll come with you.

You know that, right?

I do. And I might take you up on that.

Anytime.

Late that night, Tobyn flipped through her song book. She was originally going to have Lux record the video for her with her fancy camera, but the trolls were really starting to get to her and she just wanted to shut them up. She propped her phone up against a stack of books, and hit record.

"So a lot of you seem to think I'm a fraud, a fake, just in it for the attention. But I need you all to know that I'm one hundred percent real, so here I am."

Tobyn sang a song she'd written, belting

out lyrics that had come from deep inside her. She'd always been so afraid of someone telling her she wasn't good enough—her voice or her songs—but now, after missing out at the a cappella competition and not being picked after the Maybe Someday audition, she felt like she didn't have anything left to lose.

She played back the recording a few times and then uploaded it. Then she flipped to another page in her song book and recorded another video. And then another one. It was freeing to share her music with the world this way. It made her feel like she was in control, when everything about the past couple of months had felt completely out of her control. She wanted to make one more video before she fell asleep, but when she turned to the next page in her song book, it was a song she didn't think she was ready to record yet.

"I've been watching your videos," Devyn said.

Sabrina had told Devyn on their weekly call that Tobyn wanted to see her, and Devyn—who had a new cell phone and a new number—texted Tobyn and asked if she could meet at a coffee shop near Serenity House, her sober living home. Noelle was waiting for Tobyn around the corner at a bookstore. Tobyn felt her phone buzz and knew it was Noelle checking on her already.

"Really?" Tobyn asked.

Devyn nodded. "They're so good. You know I've always been your number one fan."

Tobyn looked down at her phone and texted Noelle a quick thumbs up.

"Look, Dev. I'm sorry for what I said at the a cappella show. But . . . why didn't you tell me what was going on with you?"

"You always saw me in this very specific way, Tobes. A good way. You saw the best of me. I didn't want to change that, and I didn't want to lose that . . . or you."

"Secrets and lies are how you lose people, Dev," Tobyn said. "I thought you were too busy for me, or that you hated me or something."

"It wasn't about you at all," Devyn said. Tobyn believed her.

"I see you're still wearing the bracelet. Even though you were mad at me," Devyn said with a smile.

Tobyn nodded. "I wanted to keep my promise to you, to keep singing. The bracelet helped me remember. I had a plan. But with everything that went down the last couple of weeks, I'm not sure what's going to happen next year at all."

Tobyn asked Devyn about rehab and how it was having a little more freedom now, and then she told her big sister all about her viral video and Maybe Someday and a cappella.

"The secret show is actually happening downtown tonight, but I wanted to see you more than I wanted to see them."

"What?" Devyn said. "You have to go!" She looked at her phone. "If you leave now, you can still catch the end of it."

"But Dev—"

"Tobes. We're good. I'm doing good. You have my new number, and we can hang out whenever you want. But you should go to that show."

"Come with me?" Tobyn asked.

Devyn shook her head. "I'm not ready for

live shows yet. Going or performing. But I saw Noelle texting you. Take her. Have fun. Go for me. I'll text you later."

At the Maybe Someday show, she and Noelle stayed close. They sang and danced and laughed, and Tobyn felt lighter than she had in weeks, even when the new band member came out on stage. The girl's name was Imani, and she was one of the few who hadn't been mean to Tobyn the day of the audition. She was as gorgeous as her big and powerful voice. She performed a ballad that slowed down the whole mood of the show, and Tobyn stepped closer to Noelle than she'd been the whole night. She grabbed her friend's hands, loving the feeling of her soft palms, her rough fingertips.

"I hope you know that kiss in the closet meant something to me," Tobyn said.

Noelle nodded. "Me too," she said.

When Tobyn kissed Noelle this time, it was out in the open. And she knew even if everything changed next year, she'd at least have been honest about this one thing. She loved her best friend, and Noelle might even love her back.

13

Tobyn hadn't been to Lee's Dumplings in months, but she knew surprising Noelle at work was one of the only ways she'd be able to get her alone. And it was important to Tobyn that they were alone when she said what she'd been planning to say for weeks, ever since she broke up with Ava.

Tobyn was nervous but focused when she pushed open the doors to the restaurant. Noelle was taking a phone order, but she glanced up when Tobyn walked in and smiled widely, finished taking the order, then walked over.

"Hey! Why didn't you tell me you were coming? Here, sit down. You want soup dumplings?"

Tobyn swallowed hard. "I didn't come by to eat. I . . . wanted to see you. To talk to you. Do you have a minute?"

Noelle glanced behind her. They weren't too busy, so Tobyn hoped she'd be able to sneak away. But Tobyn realized she'd done it again—thought about her own feelings instead of thinking about the other person's situation.

"Is everything okay?" Noelle asked. "I can't really step away right now, but if it's an emergency . . ."

"No. Sorry," Tobyn said. "You're working. Just, yeah. I'll take those dumplings. I'll hang out and wait until you can take a break?"

Noelle smiled and nodded. She pulled out a chair at the nearest table and Tobyn sat down.

A half hour later, after Tobyn had finished an order of soup dumplings and scallion pancakes, Noelle tapped her on the shoulder.

"We can talk now, if you're done eating. I'm about to take my break."

Outside on the busy Chinatown sidewalk, Tobyn reached into her bag and pulled out a folder. She'd copied the lyrics she'd written to Noelle's original composition from the fall showcase, "For You," onto sheets of music, her words floating between staffs that held the notes for the cello. Noelle opened the folder, and Tobyn watched as her eyes widened, understanding settling over her face followed quickly by joy.

"Tobyn," Noelle said. "What?!"

Tobyn laughed. "I've been working on this for a while; wanted to get it just right before I gave it to you."

When Noelle looked up, she was grinning

widely. "Okay. This is amazing. But like, why? When? How?"

"You wrote me a song first, loser," Tobyn joked.

Noelle giggled. "I guess that's true. I just . . . had no idea."

Tobyn shrugged. "I write a lot. I just don't share it much."

Noelle shook her head in disbelief. "I need to hear you sing this, you know. Like soon."

Tobyn nodded. "I'd love to. But Noelle?"

"Hmm?" Her eyes were still on the sheet music in her hands.

"I wanted to ask you . . ."

Noelle looked up.

"I know you just came out, so I will understand if you're not ready. But if you are . . . I really like you. And, I guess I'm wondering: Will you be my girlfriend?"

Noelle blushed, smiled, and nodded.

14

"Ty, get off of him!" Micah yelled to her boyfriend, who had Emmett in a headlock.

The girls chatted on Micah's roof, while the boys were play wrestling.

Noelle was sitting on the concrete floor, in front of Tobyn, who had her fingers in her girlfriend's thick curls.

"Oh, let them have their fun," Tobyn said.

"What happened with your mom when she asked why you hadn't gotten any acceptance or rejection letters, T?" Lux asked.

"Oh, she flipped out," Tobyn said. "But I

mean, there's literally nothing she can do except ground me forever, which she did, but she still has to go to work, so we'll see how grounded I actually end up being."

"But what are you going to do about next year?" Micah asked. "Noelle will be at the Manhattan School of Music, I'll be at Columbia, and Lux is gonna travel with Emmett. I don't know how she convinced *her* dad to let her go."

Tobyn had been thinking about this. "I started uploading videos like we talked about. Of me singing some of my original songs. And they aren't going viral or anything, but I like doing it way more than I expected. I think I'll keep doing that, and maybe try to hit up some open mic nights around the city. And yes, to keep my mom off my back, I'll get a job, too."

"Oh yay! So you'll still be in New York!" Micah said.

Emmett came over and hopped into Lux's lap. "Dude, you are too huge for that!"

Ty kissed Micah on the cheek, and she shoved him away. "You're so sweaty!"

Noelle leaned her head back into Tobyn's lap and grinned. "I'm just happy you'll be around."

"I'm bored," Emmett said.

"Me too," Ty agreed. "You mean to tell me the Flyy Girls don't have something crazy planned for the end of the school year?"

"Well, actually . . . ," Tobyn said.

"Oh yeah!" Micah shouted.

"Should we?" Noelle asked.

"Definitely," Lux said. "But what were we doing again?"

The Flyy Girls all laughed.

"We're crashing that party . . . ," Tobyn started to say when Lux stood up and grabbed her bag.

"Oh, I remember now," she said. "Let's go!"